Considering I was an only child, I always liked mixing and blending with children and later adults. I can make up jokes and stories about anything, so I decided to write a story and send it off to a publisher who has taken me on board. For me, a new journey has begun. Anyone who knows me and has been subjected to my humour would enjoy my writing. Ideas come to me through everyday life and my grandchildren know that I love life even when I participate with my nine-year-old granddaughter on the swings or activity corner at the park. There are plenty of romance, horror, sci-fi and action packed and everyday life stories put into books. But I've chosen a different path, for which gender doesn't matter (i.e., who chooses to read my work).

Enjoy.

My husband and family have spurred me on with encouragement and future visions of me producing many stories, of which Austin Macauley has also given me a chance to excel myself. At school, my choice of subjects was always English, literature and poetry. My thanks also for my grandson's partner, Nadia, who has been a vital wave of modern knowledge and technical advisor. Thank you all for believing in me and my work.

Barbara Ann Joyce

DEVIL ON THE DANCEFLOOR

AUSTIN MACAULEY PUBLISHERS™

LONDON · CAMBRIDGE · NEW YORK · SHARJAH

A CIP catalogue record for this title is available from the British Library.

ISBN 9781528998680 (Paperback)
ISBN 9781528998697 (ePub e-book)

www.austinmacauley.com

First Published 2023
Austin Macauley Publishers Ltd®
1 Canada Square
Canary Wharf
London
E14 5AA

Vin wished he'd never owned or needed a phone because today, it never stopped ringing. The next ring—I'm telling the caller to go jump in a river. The message counter was flashing like a beacon until Vin put a finger on the button.

"Hi Vin, it's Joe. Buzz me."

Joe answered after one ring. "Oh thank God, Vin. Do you need a job? It's well paid and guess who the employees are." Vin had already foreseen a vision of exactly who they were. "Are you there, Vin?" asked Joe, hitting a silence.

Vin had mapped out a future in business management but life wasn't so secure, and when his parents divorced, Vin and his dreams fell apart. Joe Kaplinsky and Vin were friends way back at school. Joe was sincere and could always cheer Vin up with stories about his job.

"So, are you interested the job would suit you to the ground? Please, Vin. If you think I'm pole sliding to amuse your clientele, forget it."

Vin began to laugh. "Okay, don't get your boxers in a twist. I'll call in the club tomorrow."

Vin could hear Joe saying, "Yes, yes, yes."

Personal transport was a no-go for Vin. So, a local bus was the only option, and when the driver asked, "Did you say the Star Club, Mofar Road? But that's a poofter place."

"That's exactly what I said." Vin put his fare in the slot and sat down. Joe would have flipped with the driver, but what a shock it was to find people don't or won't accept gay people!

"The morons," Vin muttered. The Star Club looked uninviting and drab. On entering the aged front door, a voice was saying, "Hi there, are you from the planning department? Give me a sec. I'll just turn the alarm off." Vin turned to face a twenty-something male who had mistaken him for someone who worked. 'If only…' Vin thought.

The young man introduced himself as Soz and invited Vin into the club.

"I'm Vin, a friend of Joe." Soz looked confused. "Joe asked me to pop in, said there was a bar manager vacancy." Vin was looking at the club's decor when voices entered the room, and suddenly he was being eyed from every angle.

"Oh hello, love. Have you come for the job? Well, ladies, shall we hire? What's your name, sweet?"

"It's Vin, and yes I've come for the job. Also, I'm waiting for my friend Joe."

Suddenly, all mouths fell open. "Any friend of Joe is good enough for us. You're hired." Joe came into the club, wondering how Vin was in the middle of the ladies.

"Joe darling, we've hired Vin. He's fabulous." Everyone introduced themselves to Vin and wished him good luck. Suddenly, a silence fell inside the club and Joe looked a shade pale.

"Are you okay, Joe? What's wrong?" This was unlike Joe. Also, the ladies were on edge when a man's menacing voice could be heard. The voice distinctly sounded angry as the words became louder, and on hearing, "Lady whores, get to work," Vin angered and said, "who the hell is that?"

Joe said, "It's okay, Vin. It's the Furor; he runs the club. Take no notice." But Vin felt a disturbance in Joe.

On entry, the voice materialised into a six-foot muscular male whose stance looked threatening. The laser-beam stare at Vin was unmistakable. "Joe, have you forgotten the club rules? No socialising in worktime."

But before Joe could answer, Vin walked over to the loudmouthed hulk and said, "It's okay, no need to bawl at Joe. I popped in to see if the bar vacancy was still available."

Suddenly, the faceoff turned in a different direction when the Furor became Mr Nice Guy.

"Oh, take no notice. Everyone knows I'm a stickler for everything, especially when one's back is turned." Upstairs, everyone was jumping with joy at what they had listened to, the Furor being face-to-face with someone who didn't give a shit about who he was. Everyone scattered at the sound of footsteps slamming up the staircase. Everyone looked busy as the door opened.

"Okay, my little faggot pussies, any visits to the club are to be approved by me. Is that understood?" He warned, poking a long, sharp-nailed finger into everyone's chest. Then last of all came the threat as usual. "Oh, by the way, I've taken on some security. Anyone wishing to go against me or my rules will need to think again." Bitchy saw the grey sick-to-the-stomach look on everyone's face. "That's it. Time to seek help or get the hell out of here, never to return."

As the Furor put his hand on the doorknob, he turned and reminded the ladies the club will be closed for refurbishment for one week only and be here for the opening or else…

"He's one sadistic bastard," said Witchy. The door flew open so quick.

BANG! The Furor had slammed Witchy so hard into the wall; there was blood splattered everywhere. "Like I said, go against me and faggots will be crying." He released Witchy and left the club as if nothing had occurred. Raggy put a cold compress on Witchy's head.

Soz came through the door. "What the hell's going on? That bastard's gone too far. Let's get Witchy to hospital fast."

Vin had left the club uneasy, knowing that something was seriously wrong. The ladies were upset. As for Joe, he would get a grilling and spill the beans to Vin about what really was going on at the club.

Soz phoned for a taxi and accompanied Witchy to A&E. Upon entry in the hospital, a nurse came over. She knew the ladies from the club because when the nurses wanted a good fun night out for a celebration, the Star Club was the place to go.

Sally was a good nurse, kind and thoughtful.

"What's happened to your head and face? Did you walk into a wall?"

Bitchy muttered, "More like walked into a hard fist." Raggy and Soz gave Bitchy the say-no-more look.

"It's okay, love. We'll get you sorted out in no time." Nurse Sally and her colleagues had been to the club many times for birthdays or a hen night. It occurred to her that nightclub injuries usually happened late at night, not early afternoon. Witchy was waiting in a cubicle to be checked when a wall of eyes peered around the curtain.

"Oh my God! It's Witchy. The nurses must have ditched their patients to see him."

The doctor quickly assessed Witchy, just a dressing and clean up. "Any problems, come back." But who would be coming back next? After the doctor gave Witchy the all-clear, the nurses said goodbye and promised they would come to the club soon. The nurses were friends and at lunchbreak, they became detectives.

Sally spliced out, "Guess what? My Bruv is a cop." June and Beth had their jaws dropped.

Sally laughed when Beth said, "Oh, and didn't I tell you my father is a magistrate at the local law courts? I'll run the club owner's name by him to see if any alarm bells ring." Jane mentioned that her nanna used to work at the Star Club as a cleaner. She remembered her nanna didn't stay there long. In fact, she described the boss as a people-hater and a sadistic bastard, and her nanna never swore.

Joe buzzed Soz. "Where is everyone? We've job applicants to deal with. Just get to the club ASAP." The phone went dead. The club was soon to be closed for refurbishment and upgrade. Joe's mind was whirling; new staff was needed, i.e., a new DJ to get the place rocking, a regular cabaret artist and bar staff. 'Hopefully, Vin will accept the bar manager position. He would be perfect. Vacancies were posted online and in the local press. Fingers crossed, the right people will apply. Hopefully, the Furor won't upset anyone.'

Vin had a text from old friends – Chris and Rudi.

"Hi, Vin, how would you and some friends like to come over for a gay old time? Let us know."

Vin smiled at the phrase 'gay old time'.

'Trust me to be the straight one.' Vin loved all his friends, straight or gay. 'That I can live with, but no job or money, I can't,' he thought.

Joe buzzed Vin to ask if he had considered the bar vacancy. With shock, Joe heard the immortal words, "Yes, I'll take it."

Joe muttered, "Thank you, Lord."

"It's Vin, not the Lord." They both laughed.

"Okay, mate. See you soon." The ladies began preparations for the last night at the club before its closure.

Joe was interviewing a pretty girl who was slightly shy but wanted the singing job. "What's your name, love?"

"It's Ally."

"Okay, Ally, the stage is yours."

'Oh my God!' thought Joe.

She sang 'Walking on Sunshine', and God only knew it was the only sunshine in the club. Ally sang like an angel and everyone gave her applause, and all agreed she was hired. A sudden noise erupted; it was the Furor. A word Bitchy and Soz. Raggy had goosebumps.

"Didn't I fucking say no one was to come here unless I authorise it? So who the hell is she?"

Joe spoke up, "Her name is Ally and she applied for the singing vacancy."

"So why do you want the vacancy?" asked the moronic Furor.

"Because I need a job and some money, as I can't live on fresh air, not that there's much of that in here. Also, I don't remember a queue outside for the job."

Raggy whispered that she'd got balls, so the Furor could take it or leave it. The Furor disappeared, and Joe was interviewing the next applicant. This interview went well. It was for a DJ.

"So what's your setup called?"

"Just call me Blue Light."

"Okay, Blue Light, we look forward to seeing you soon." Joe shook hands, pleased with securing a DJ and a singer for the closing night. The Furor had requested the ladies, or bitches as he spitefully spat out, to assemble in ten minutes for a meeting. Joe had to bite his tongue from replying, "Yes sir—no sir, anything else, you living abortion."

Witchy piped up, "Come on, girls. We've hit the skids. What's new?"

A rumble-like thunder materialised as the Furor and his personal security entered the room, making knees and teeth shake. "Okay, you overgrown pussies, listen up and listen good. Friday night we'll close up. I want every door gushing with clients fighting to get in my club. Give them a night they won't forget, comprendez faggots."

The ladies had put a plan together for the night's entertainment until the Furor said, "Stop right there." He wasn't happy about the male dance troupe.

"Who are they?" he asked, threatening. Heads rolled.

Thinking out loud, Soz muttered, "What's new?"

"Was that a little moan or do you want to get whipped with the cream?"

"So, who is lined up for the cabernet evening?"

Raggy replied to Furor, "They had DJ Blue Light doing the disco, Ally the singer and the male dancers."

Furor spat out, "And don't disappoint me or else…" Vin must have come into the club and heard the Furor.

"Hi everyone, who would like to get away from this place?" asked Vin.

Raggy, Bitchy Witchy, Soz and Joe practically pounced on Vin. "Yes, yes. Just say the word, in fact purgatory sounds friendlier than this shithole." Friday came so quickly. The club was ready to give the regulars a good time. The DJ set the sound system up. Then Ally came in to check the microphone system was working. All seemed well, and Soz noticed how chatty Ally and Blue Light were. Ally casually asked where the boss was. Then Blue Light enquired who the heavies were and why they were here now and not later when the club opened. Ally was now asking how long the Boss had been running the club, unaware that his adopted name was the Furor. Soz had been put on the spot with awkward questions, so quickly he pretended he had a phone call to make.

Some hours later, the club doors were ready to be opened up for the last night. There were faces the ladies didn't recognise. After tonight, who cared anyway? Joe was praying that Vin would be too busy behind the bar to notice if the Furor was his normal evil self. Vin would kick the crap out of him for sure. Ally hit the stage after the dancers and everyone engaged more. Blue Light hit the sound barrier with his Ibiza party tunes and the club rocked. The nurses from A&E were calling to the ladies to join them. Nurse Sally introduced her brother and said, "We've dragged him out for some fun."

Her brother asked, "Who are the heavies on the door?"

Bitchy said, "They are the bouncers the Furor has hired."

"Who's the Furor?" asked her brother.

Soz quickly ushered them to the bar before beans were spilt. Even Ally asked the whereabouts of Mr Mean Machine. 'Who cares?' Soz thought. 'The club is on the countdown to close.' Blue light played the last music to the chants of 'We Want More'. A voice growled out to get them all out as quick as possible.

"… And you all come to my office when everyone has gone." The Furor had materialised from nowhere. The ladies just wanted out of here and quick. The club emptied, and all were waiting for the impact from the Furor. "So, faggots, who's been in this office searching and ransacking my filling cabinets."

The ladies were fearful when Joe answered, "No one. I repeat: no one has left the downstairs area for any reason, as we have all been busy."

The Furor said nothing and walked away. Everyone collected the belongings and, putting two fingers up, said, "To hell, you rotten pig." And all left the club like prisoners released from some hellhole prison.

Two days later, Joe rang Vin to confirm everyone was packed and ready to spend a weekend away. Rudi and Chris knew Vin and Joe from way back, and Joe hoped they knew what they were taking on inviting the ladies for a weekend.

The banging and clattering sound of voices and doors slamming awoke Rudi and Chris. "Oh shit! It can't be them already." Chris jumped out of bed, grabbing his beloved pink boa dressing gown and cursed when he stubbed his toe. "I'm coming. I'm coming." He opened the door with a quizzical look. Bitchy asked if they had called at the wrong moment. Everyone was bursting to laugh at the pink boa dressing gown.

Soz said, "I like your mules. They match your d—." Too late, everyone busted out laughing.

Rudi shouted from upstairs, "What's going on down there? Sounds like an orgy on a turkey farm!"

The ladies shouted back, "How did you know, gobble gobble?" Joe asked if there were any rich people or celebrities around these parts.

Chris responded quickly with: "We were the only gays in the village till you woodheads arrived." Chris and Rudi were a fun couple and easy-to-like guys. Everyone was introduced and welcomed, and Chris asked what the ladies had planned for the weekend.

"Joe knows what we're like, all organised, and if there's a spanner in the works, it sets us in a spasm."

Witchy and Soz laughed. "We'd all have a spasm on the end of any spanner, darling." Everyone had a good breakfast, and plans were made about where to go and what to do to keep them occupied for the weekend.

Back at the club, refurbishment hadn't begun, and what was the hurry to close up? Alex Alburn aka DJ Blue was a CID officer with the local police force, who had decided to return to the club and check it and its staff out. Banging on the front door, Alex could hear voices inside when the door opened by a burly man. "What do you want?" he snapped at Alex.

"I left some disco equipment. I'll collect it if that's okay."

The hulk said, "Wait there. What's your name?"

"Tell the boss it's DJ Blue. He'll know."

The hulk growled to Alex, "The boss ain't here." This info surprised Alex. There were no sounds like drilling, banging or any visual signs or workmen to confirm any refurbishment work.

The hulk opened a door and said, "Get your stuff and get out." Purposely, Alex had left a couple of old speakers as an excuse to return to the club. Some voices were heard from the stairs.

Alex could hear part of a conversation, "You got two days to bring the money, and if any sniff is missing, you're dead. Now go!"

A voice shouted at Alex, "Are you ready to leave?"

Quickly, Alex replied, "Sorry, buddy, some idiots moved the equipment. I'll just check the cellar." It was more like a rubbish dump with alcohol and all sorts of crap. Then he took a quick visit upstairs and into the Furor's office – which looked like a crime scene. There was blood around the walls; no doubt the ladies had been bashed and assaulted here. There was white dust all over the floor, and from habit, Alex wet his finger to dab it up and sniffed and tasted it.

'Oh hell!' he thought. 'It's cocaine, alright, and whatever this place is hiding, I'm putting a stop to it.'

The two heavies returned with two speakers. "Is this what you came for?" He pushed them onto Alex and said, "Don't come back again." Slam went the door. The speakers had a white dust over them, which Alex took to the police forensic lab where Tony, the techno officer, set up the swab-tested.

"Come back later, Alex. I'll get you some results." Alex reported to his boss, and a plan was put into place about the club. Back at Chris and Rudi's house, everyone had shopping plans. They went into town like children with pocket money. Sometime later and laden with gifts, the thought of a cup of tea was sheer heaven.

Upstairs, Joe had noticed a bedroom door ajar, and Rudi was sitting on the bed, looking sad and subdued. Joe tapped on the door. "Everything okay, Rudi? Everyone's out in the garden, so spill. I know you're not your vacuous self. What's wrong?"

Wiping away a tear, Rudi began with: "Two weeks ago, my mother passed away."

Joe put an arm around him. "Why didn't you tell anyone?"

"The thing is she knew I was gay. She never questioned me. Always reassured me in everything I did. She always made my friends welcome and always told me she loved me no matter what."

"Now listen up, we are your friends. We've all been to hell and back."

Rudi added, "But my father doesn't know, and he wouldn't understand, and if he knew I was gay or as he says, a shirt lifter, it would kill him. My father is an overbearing, mental, abusing bastard and I wish he were dead." Chris had felt unhappiness from the ladies when they arrived and now was the perfect time to decide their future.

"Vin, what you thinking?" asked Raggy. "You are miles away."

"I'm thinking we should all get dressed up this evening and pop in the village pub for some drinks, if anyone's interested." The queue for a shower and a buz which Vin had not heard for a while had begun.

Vin asked, "Shall I order some champagne, as freedom needs to be celebrated?"

Soz chirped up, "Fuck the champagne. Just order plenty of slag juice; we love it."

Vin laughed, "Okay, slag juice it is."

The local taxi service was happy to take everyone to the pub and was booked for later when everyone would be well and truly pissed and staggering.

The chitchat and drinks were flowing when Raggy said, "Wow, friends, take a look outside." A mini bus with a selection of good-looking fit males on board had parked outside. They all entered the pub, obviously happy. They were Leeds United fans, and a burger and a pint was needed to refuel them. Eye contact began, and the ladies were ecstatic. Joe was in his element as he had been a Leeds' fan at school. A fan called Steve said hello and asked, "Are you all celebrating?"

He listened to accounts of what everyone had been through at the club. He looked gutted and said that he wished he and the lads had known everyone before, as they would have sorted the Furor and his thugs out. Steve and his friends departed with a piece of sadness. Also, it was time for the ladies' departure. The taxis were ready and waiting. Vin was drunk as a skunk, with mumbles and stumbles. As for the ladies, did they give a flying fuck? Definitely not.

The next morning was headaches and hangovers, and the thought of packing and moving on to a new life was easier said than done.

Over breakfast and coffee, Rudi and Chris expressed their good luck wishes and asked everyone in town what their new life plans were.

"Okay, Raggy, spill."

Raggy, a.k.a Raggan Delois, announced, "I'm returning to Jamaica to my family and a previous romance I won't ever walk away from again."

"Wow!" said Joe. "Okay, Witchy, your turn."

Witchy, a.k.a William Witchelier, said, "My brother and his wife have just had their first baby. They live in New York. They run a bar and things are getting heavy, so I've offered to help them. My plane tickets are booked. Oh, and Soz, a.k.a Filipe Sozlosky, will be joining me, so *asta la vista,* everyone."

"So what clientele use this bar?" asked Vin.

Witchy winked and said, "Does gay ring any bells?"

"Okay, Vin, so what's your new life plan?" asked Rudi.

"I'm actually thinking of becoming a police officer."

"Wow! We didn't see that one coming," said everyone.

"Last of all, Joe, come on, spill quick and fast," said Vin.

"Come on, Joe, who's the lucky male in your life? Don't keep us in suspenders," said Soz.

Nervously, Joe said, "Sorry, girls, it's not a man. It's a she, a very gentle caring and understanding girl. I kept my love for her a secret. I've never felt this way for anyone but her." Everyone had a tear in their eyes.

"Hell, who cares?" said Chris, "As long as you're happy. In fact, as long as we are all happy, good luck to you all and God be with you. *Au revoir."*

On returning home, Vin messaged Detective Alex Albarn to meet up for a coffee if and when he was free. Two days later, an email arrived from Alex to say he was on a course and would be happy to meet up and praised Vin for his choice of career. Vin and Alex met up at the local coffee shop.

"It's good to see you, and I'm happy everyone has moved on to new lives." Alex didn't know who was doing what until Vin put him in the picture. "Alex, your mouth just fell open. You are as surprised as I were when Joe told me he was in love with a girl, not a man." Vin relayed what everyone had chosen to do and Alex was happy for them. "Vin, mate, I've got to shoot. Please email me when you hear from the Met because we are celebrating bigtime." A couple of weeks later, a letter which accepted and approved of Vin to become a police officer had arrived, and another chapter for Vin began. Some weeks later, just before the police training began, Alex and Ally contacted him with some disturbing news.

"It's your friends Rudi and Chris." Vin's mind couldn't keep still; 'Rudi and Chris, what are they up to now? They were selling their house last I knew.' Ally was obviously upset and told Vin that the pair had been targeted by some bloodthirsty, psychotic haters who had set fire to their house, and the flames were so fast and fierce that they were trapped and the inevitable happened.

Vin felt physically sick and shocked to the core. "I and Ally are investigating, and we won't leave a stone unturned. We will find the bastards who took Rudi and Chris out, and that's a promise. Be in touch soon." There was a shake of the hand from Alex and a tear and kiss from Ally. Returning home, Vin couldn't think which way or how he could break this nightmare to everyone, but they all have to know what had occurred to Chris and Rudi.

A heartbroken silence from Soz, Witchy, Raggy and Joe spoke unsaid words. Vin managed to sort out a funeral package.

"For Chris and Rudi, and bless everyone they sent a substantial amount of money by cheque to pay for their send-off. Until Alex got under way with the investigation." Vin could only promise to keep all up to date with any news. The investigation revealed that Maxton Veener had a daughter who was part of a sadistic pact that murdered Chris and Rudi.

It appeared she knew of the club and its employees, and Daddy Furor had told her the ladies had robbed him of money and cocaine. Daddy had told her to get them where it hurt most. That definitely worked, and Alex told how she knew of Rudi and Chris. After the weekend of fun and relaxation, all was back to normal. Rudi and Chris had decided to put their house up for sale and move nearer to the city. The Furor's daughter had posed as a possible buyer. The ladies had been spied on, and luckily, the estate agent had taken a photograph on his phone of the female, and a puzzle fell into place. Alex's investigation was closing in.

"The daughter was married to a local businessman who we are also checking out. It appears the bitch travels frequently, i.e., New York, Mexico and not family holidays either." Vin wanted to begin his police training ASAP to catch the fucked up murderers as quick as possible. Hopefully, Daddy and his little girl will holiday at Her Majesty's holiday hotel: HMP Forever. Vin had opted for the metropolitan force as its central location would be ideal for Heathrow when everyone came to visit, hopefully not until this filthy shit was sorted out. Vin was settled with his police training, and what made him strong in mind and determination was the memory of Chris and Rudi. Alex was a good mentor and when Vin's last two weeks had finally ended a promise from Alex that they would meet up and, as Alex put it, get sloshed, pissed or fucking smashed. Everyone sent good luck messages. There was also an invitation from Witchy and Soz to get his arse on a plane for New York. One part of the training mentally hurt Vin, enacting the scenario of finding bodies brutally stabbed or burnt to unrecognition in a housefire. The training sergeant hadn't seen Vin look sick or upset before.

"Are you okay?" he asked. Vin apologised for letting personal trauma sway him.

The sergeant said, "Vin wasn't the first or last trainee to be affected, and he would grow stronger with experience. Joe liked the idea of going to New York for his stag party. What better plan than a knees-up at Witchy's bar, gays, straights mixing and blending, and Raggy's threat of doing a comedy evening? It's got to be done." Alex emailed Vin to meet up.

"It's important."

Vin had that sick gut feeling. 'Hell, let's see what's up.' Alex had that police look on his face. Vin's stomach turned.

"Okay, Vin, the good news is the Furor and his daughter have both been charged with murder and supplying 'Class A' drugs plus some other bad shit. The case has been thoroughly investigated and the daughter's husband is charged with dealing and selling arms, of which all will be imprisoned for a long time. As for the club, I know for a fact it's being demolished."

"Thank you, Alex. I will let everyone know. You're a good cop. I hope I'm as good and professional as you some day." Everyone's spirit lifted on knowing the outcome of the Furor and his daughter, and a new feeling of happiness swept a new vibe into their hearts and souls. Meeting Joe and Raggy at Heathrow felt good. It was busy, and some rowdy travellers at the bar suddenly materialised as the Leeds supporters Vin and everyone met when they stayed at Chris and Rudi's.

"Hi, Steve. Don't tell me Leeds is playing in New York."

"No mate, it's my sixtieth, and we are celebrating large."

Steve's mate Jimmy said, "This lot don't celebrate the dicks, just go on an alcoholic rampage."

Joe said, "That's my kinda party."

"What are you going to New York for?" asked Steve.

"It's my stag do, and Raggy here is the stand-up comedy at our friends' bar." The meetup for Steve's 60th and Joe's stag night was arranged.

Steve asked Vin if he was okay.

"Yes, it is now." And he told of Chris and Rudi's demise and the outcome.

"I'm sorry, Vin, for you and your friends. You will always remember them."

"We will for sure."

Jimmy asked Steve, "Was it sensible to meet up at a gay bar knowing what meatheads the footie lads were, especially when sozzled?" The flight was surprisingly smoothe and quiet. Witchy had let Vin know the bar he and Soz were helping out with was changing over to him soon. His brother had realised that running a busy bar and parenting a new baby was all too much. The clientele were great and were happy that Witchy and Soz were taking over. Letting Raggy loose with stand-up humour would determine numbers of customers. The day of reckoning was upon them.

Joe wondered, 'Is this the right choice of stag party?' as the customers began to arrive. A couple of guys came in cop uniforms. What friendly welcoming people were saying hi to Vin, Joe and Raggy.

Raggy asked, "Is it fancy dress, Witchy?"

"No, they really are cops." That shut him up. Steve, Jimmy and the lads walked in. The present customers thought it was Christmas Day and heaven all in one. Raggy was on the microphone; everyone was listening up.

"Witchy, could you make two cocktails? One for Steve. He's sixty, everyone." A wail of 'happy birthday' came. "Also, a cocktail for Joe. He's getting married." Another cheer came. Then Witchy asked which cocktail they wanted.

A male dressed in bike leathers said, "Give them a *peniscolada.*"

"It's not much to look at, okay, to put your lips round."

Laughter poured out through the night.

"Yes, Joe, you made the right decision to come to New York." Vin also told Steve who wholeheartedly agreed.

"What do you think, Jimmy?"

"I'd say absolute fucking madness, but we're all happy. Witchy and Soz gave drinks on the house. To penises all over, cheers."

Vin wasn't quite sure what he was feeling happy with his new career or was it loneliness? Someone suggested, "Get a pet, anything you can talk to other than yourself."

"What pet would feel company with a lonely cop until the woman of his dreams turns up."

A colleague at the force suggested a trip to the local animal shelter, which Vin halfheartedly did.

"Were you looking for any particular pet? Dog, rabbit, hamster?" the lady asked. In a corner, an area which housed cats and kittens came into view. Vin was watching two springy playful felines who made Vin smile. One was teasing the other.

'Oh my God, they remind me of Chris and Rudi.'

Vin asked if they were up for adoption.

The lady said, "Yes but only as a pair." Vin's heart decided, and the paperwork was processed. The shelter staff was so happy that their long-stay lodgers were being rehomed to someone they knew was the right person.

Vin had already decided they were to be given new names – Rudi and Chrissy. Everyone emailed Vin happy at his pets' names. The arrangement to collect Chrissy and Rudi didn't happen as a knock on Vin's door changed things.

"Ally, is it really you?"

"Come in."

"Are you okay?"

Vin was aghast. "What have you got here taking a travel box with something inside from Ally. I believe you've adopted these fun creatures. Can I let them out?"

"Sure you can. I arranged to collect them myself from the shelter." Rudi and Chrissy located to the sofa like it was their comfort zone.

"Where have you been, Ally? I haven't had any contact from you. I was thinking all sorts, plus I didn't ask Alex."

"Vin, I'm really sorry. Believe me, I've turned my life around. One minute, the police was all I ever wanted to do then wam— I'd had enough. I volunteered at the shelter and they employed me. I love it. I asked Alex not to tell you. I'm truly sorry, Vin." A deep conversation followed, and a new relationship between them looked promising. Vin put his arms around her and kissed her with a promise that he would be there for her and his friends whenever. Back to life and back to reality, Vin was a fulltime police officer. His new boss allocated his duty roster at a known gay community.

"This is right up my street and I know our friends Chris and Rudi would be happy for me. Come what may, straight or gay, I will always ensure justice is done to all."

A new day began for Vin with lots of post emails from Witchy and also an email from Alex who was relocating himself and his job to a small coastal town.

"It's lively, Vin, but quiet when the holiday season is over and my new home is minutes from the beach." Alex put, *"Haha! I must be getting old."*

Vin's reply was:

"So there's plenty of beach babes. Then you watch this space. I'm moving there. Ha!"

Witchy's email was a request and surprise.

"Hi Vin, hope you're okay and settled in your job. We are fine, but the bar is quiet. I've pulled hair. I've got out. Do you think Ally would want to sing for us at the bar? It needs an infusion. She sang like an angel at the Star Club, if it's okay with you."

"Wow, what a bombshell, okay. Witchy, I'll put your offer to her."

Joe and Roselle had set a date for their wedding, and thankfully, it would be here in London where everyone could meet up for a get-together. When Raggy was asked about his future status, his reply was, "I've had enough of women and

I'm waiting for Mr Right to come along." Joe advised him to make his fucking mind up and look into a mirror sometime. Since Joe's stag party in New York, Raggy felt he wasn't as happy as he thought. So, once and for all, his mind was made up.

"I'm getting a visa, and if Witchy will have me at the bar, I'll do comedy nights, fingers crossed." Talk amongst the officers at Vin's cop shop was that of local teens physically and verbally abusing the community where Vin was assigned. On the evening shift, Vin had no choice but to patrol his community, of which some scumbag teenagers were hassling and throwing missiles at any males entering the local bar.

"I'm not letting this go any further. I'm calling for backup."

But a piercing male voice rang out, and this sounded serious. A teen girl was screaming and shouting, "Someone, help! He's been stabbed." The welcome sound of sirens came, but Vin was applying CPR to the young man who was bleeding intensely. Another older male had been attacked also but luckily was not on his side. The ambulance crew assured Vin that the teen looked worse than he was, but the older male didn't make it. Statements from locals stated that as the young man approached the bar, a group of teens were shouting abuse, calling him a gay boy, etc. At that moment, a male came out of the bar and told them to clear off. But an arm jerk was seen knifing him, and when he fell to his knees, the teen said, "This is our turf; no gays or your bum boys allowed," and then ran off. The officers had been given the name of the knife attacker, and reports said he was causing trouble around the area constantly.

An elderly resident told an officer, "We all knew something like this was going to happen." A woman appeared in front of Vin, shouting and bawling that had the police did their fucking job and not let queers into the bar, then her son wouldn't be in hospital. Vin wanted to put a hand around her throat and squeeze until she couldn't breathe.

"Well, madam, get your facts together because if the queer your referring to hadn't had come out the bar when he did, your son would be dead. He took the brunt of homophobic hate to protect your son and a six-inch blade, but unfortunately, the kindhearted queer died." Vin's final sentence was, "But I'm happy your son has lived, and the police will do all in their power to turn this estate around, possibly make people realise that gay people and queers are humans made of flesh and blood like you."

The woman was totally dried up for words – mission accomplished.

Back at the station, the cops all patted Vin on the shoulder. "Well done, mate." All Vin wanted to do was get home for a shower and tell his furry housemates what a shit day he'd had. After a meal and a meltdown chat with Joe, who was so happy and counting down the weeks to his wedding, what was the line-up for Vin's future? What had changed Ally? No contact was there, only: "Hi, are you okay?"

"I can't accept Witchy's offer, as I'm totally tied up at the moment. Pity she wasn't tied up to a thornbush. Why don't I try being a penis-pecker like Raggy suggested the old dreadlock bastard." Since Joe's stag party and the Leeds lads were celebrating Steve's 60th, the bar slowly went quiet and regulars asked the whereabouts of the Rasta comedian and those well, fit males. Witchy didn't want to fail his new position and let down his brother. He also needed help when things got a bit naughty with regulars, as there was no door security at all. The cops including Vin had been told the police dignitary was visiting their station in a couple of days. The sergeant stressed that all must wear full uniform and to be on duty one hour before their shift began.

"Who's this person?" Vin asked a colleague.

"Er, well, we not sure, just to look smart."

On the day, Vin's colleagues seemed different. At 9:30, Vin walked toward the briefing room, noticing colleagues giving nods and walking in front of Vin.

"Your seat's on the front row, Vin. Speak to you later, mate."

There was a silence before the sergeant began a speech, saying, "It isn't easy being a police officer, and no day is the same but we do our job to the best of our ability as Officer Vin Zeltique knows." Vin's jaw dropped, and all eyes were on him. "A young man has thankfully recovered and is back to life after a knife attack almost ended his life. The quick action of Officer Zeltique to give young Freddy CPR was to give his life extra mileage. If you would like to come up and receive your colleagues' thanks and gratitude, also the residents of the named estate have realised we are there to help them in any way we can." And all stood up to clap Vin, who got a tear and a lump with disbelief. The sergeant shook Vin's hand and requested Vin to pop to his office in ten mins.

'What could the sarge want me for?' The mother of Freddy whose life Vin had partly saved stood up when Vin entered the office.

"This is Mrs Jallow. I believe you met on the estate. Please take a seat, Vin." The woman came over to Vin visually upset and began an apology. "I'm very, very sorry and apologise to you for speaking to you with accusation and hate. My son Freddy told me he went to that bar as they were advertising for a glass collector and the money would help us. The attacker had hassled Freddy and his mates each time they were out and seeing my son come out of the bar, was screaming at him if he a gay boy now and snapped with hate, then lunged at him with a knife. Between that kindhearted man who absorbed the attackers' hatred and you for putting breath and life back into my son, thank you."

With that, she put a kiss on Vin's cheek and once again gave thanks. "Okay, Vin, take a couple of days off; have a breather. Vin asked who the male was who died. His name was Mike Sezalle, and he wasn't gay at all, not that it mattered if he wasn't. You both did good. In fact, he was a friend, a retired cop. We've had a few beers at that bar and God knows I've been hit on a few times, not that I'd minded if you get my drift. Okay, Vin, go, go, go. Take care."

In the last email from Alex, he offered Vin to pop down here for a break.

"You definitely won't want to return to London. At the time, things were quiet with his job and life. But now things and feelings had changed so it I'm going and the cats are going as well."

A text to Alex said:

"Hi okay. If I and my furry companions come, I'm in need of a break and a few beers."

The reply was:

"Get packing. See you soon. A couple of days would change me up a bit. The feel of sand on a beach. What more could I want possibly someone to share the experience with and it could have been Ally but you go forward in life and that's my new itinerary."

Chrissy and Rudi were settled in their travel carriers. He sent a quick message to Joe, Witchy and Raggy to let them know what he was up to, as it was like having three mothers. All wished Vin well.

"Do everything you're not supposed to, like get pissed every night and find a woman or a man for that matter and fucking get laid."

"The sick nutters, but hell, I'm doing all their suggestions; here we go." Arriving at the seaside address, Vin felt relaxed and it looked as if Alex had made the right choice. The house door opened.

"Hi, Vin, who's in the pet carriers?"

"They are my housemates – Chrissy and Rudi."

"Did you just say your friends' names?"

"Yes, and when I saw them messing about and teasing each other, they reminded me so much of Chris and Rudi that I just had to rehome them from the animal shelter."

"Bring them in with your stuff and I'll make us a nice cup of coffee."

"So what's with Ally may I ask?"

"Alex, I really don't know we were getting along fine. She made me feel happy. Perhaps I got too far ahead of myself. I don't know. In fact, now I've mentally deleted her and she can go fuck herself."

"I knew she had become a ghost if you like and I didn't want to poke my nose in your relationship—you've got a life, Vin. Live it, as I'm sure you will."

Vin noticed lots of traffic coming into the area where Alex lived. "Oh, Vin, I forgot to say this weekend the sea croft pride festival is on. You might get lucky, plenty of hustle bustle and lots of muscle."

"Alex, don't start that shit. I usually end up arguing or wanting to batter some asshole when they start shouting about gays."

"Well, if that's the case, I'll back you up. Been a long time since my knuckles fell on gay-hater twats."

He sent a text to Raggy.

"Guess what, Rags. I'm attending a pride festival this weekend, pity you can't be here. Just think of me eyeing up the talent. Don't it make you sick and jealous? Ha, ha!"

There was a quick reply from Raggy:

"Yes, Vin, it does make me jealous. Wait till I get my hands on you, bitch."

"Okay, Rags, I can't wait. I really must get you a swearing app, ha!"

"What the fuck is a swearing app?"

"Well, mate, when you tell bad jokes or start swearing, it will say, 'Raggy, shut the fuck app,' ha!"

"Okay, Vin, my friend, have a good time. Give Chrissy and Rudi a cuddle for me. Take care."

Downing a few beers after a great meal, which Alex cooked like a chef, Vin asked, "Are you really truly happy, Alex?"

He replied, "Yes, I am, but sometimes I feel pushed to the edge and I think to myself that I'm single, no partner, no wife... How the fuck would I... could I cope if I had. What about you?"

Vin agreed. "Policework can be rewarding, but like you, I feel confused as to is this my career till I retire or what? I feel I'm solely doing this for Chris and Rudi."

"Look, buddy, you don't have to prove nothing to nobody. You have built-in strength and adrenaline in your balls. Did I really just say that?"

Vin pulled Alex from the sofa. "Time for bed before we both wobble, but as I've got adrenaline in me balls, I won't wobble." They both laughed and clinked glasses.

"Night, mate."

"Night, buddy."

Witchy and Soz were happy and buzzin' running the New York Bar, and now Witchy had signed the paperwork to be the official owner. Things seemed to have gone quiet since a recent bar brawl. With no security, there were not many customers.

"What has gone wrong? I wish Vin was here, and this mode footie lads, they would bring the regulars back in no time."

Soz suggested, "If things got really quiet, why don't we put on a male strip show like the full monty? What do you think?"

"For a start, I wouldn't want to look at your body parts, and mine are no better. The only audience we'd get would be

34

blind and deaf, which would mean they wouldn't have to listen to our peckers banging about."

"A good idea, Soz, no more please." The pride festival was underway. The weather was great and Vin just decided he wanted to stay here and not go back to London. "Alex still does his job, just relocated here. Why didn't I think of that? But it's never too late and my options are open."

"What do you think, Vin? This festival brings people from all over. I tell you what. I think I love it here. You'll have to threaten me to leave, or else it is a great place." Alex ushered Vin behind some cars.

"What's up? Is something wrong?"

"No, Vin, cast your eyes to the float with uniforms on. I'm pretty sure that's your sergeant frolicking about up there. What would the officers say at your station if they see him on a pride float?"

"It could be worse, Alex. It could be the fantastic four—Witchy, Soz, Joe and Raggy; at least they're open about themselves."

"I would never have guessed about the sarge. He's always so prim and proper, but actually I remember now we were discussing, the bar stabbing said the older male was a friend and they had a few beers at the bar and he got hit on like he didn't mind the lying twat."

Alex suggested, "Well, if you ever need time off, just accidentally on purpose say, 'Do you know what? I saw your double at the sea croft Pride Festival.' You'll get it straight away and you'll let him know you know he's not as straight as a line prop."

"So what's the crime rate like here? I couldn't imagine it's high."

"Well, Vin, there's crime even here, which seems a normal and quiet place, but there are the regular offenders keeping the local station and myself in a job. It's not as stressful as London, but I don't go home worn out mentally, so that's a bonus."

"Okay, Vin, any more questions? As my mouth is dry and there's this quaint little pub nearby. I promise we won't get sozzled. We can get a meal there as well."

"That sounds great, just one more question."

Alex muttered, "For fuck's sake, what? Is there any crumpet here. By that, you mean nice girls. Or females, then yes. In fact, Vin, I've been dating a lovely girl. She works in the local bakery. Her name's Tia. I don't even ask for my snacks. She knows exactly what I have and like and she's not a bad cook either; bless her. She's shown me other ingredients other than pizza pot noddle and takeouts."

Vin was happy for Alex and asked, "Would Tia have any mates who would be interested in a good-looking mu-scly, who can't cook and snores in his sleep, boring cop?"

"Vin, mate, you've got more chance of a date with a corpse."

Vin's polite reply was: "Thanks, you bastard. I love you too. Joe and Roselle's wedding was fast approaching, and Vin needed to get togged up with a new suit and other items, plus not forgetting a wedding gift, of what Vin had no idea. The local pub was a friendly place and Alex was obviously liked."

"Well, eat when you're ready. The steaks are delicious."

Vin laughed. "Okay, connoisseur, let's eat. My gut is doing a military two step." Visitors from the festival were filling up the local chip shop and inside and out of the pub was busy.

"I thought this place was going to be like a small off the beaten track village. It's really cosy but lively, Alex. I do envy you. This couple of days away has recharged my batteries. The cats have adapted to Alex's sofa and house. Perhaps I should do the same."

The beach was near and Alex was called into work to cover for a colleague. "A walk and a thought might point me in the right direction when I return home. I'll be home after lunch. Help yourself to food."

Vin cheekily said, "I might pop into that bakery you mentioned."

"Okay, wise arse, you do that and get me something. Bye, mate."

Vin could smell the bakery before he got near where the smiley girls were chitchatting. They stopped when Vin and another customer entered.

"Hi, what can I get you?"

"Every pie and pastry in the shop would be nice... er... a cheese slice and some ham salad sandwiches would do nicely," the girl asked, with a doughnut for afters.

Vin knew she had talked him into it. "Yes, that as well. Are you on holiday or just a day visit?" Vin was visibly trying to read the girl's name pin.

"Er... yes, just a couple of days at my friends, which reminds me I've got orders to take him a snack as well. He said Tia knows exactly what his snack requirements were." Tia was exactly as nice and welcoming as Alex described her. Tia asked if Alex was at home; only she had phoned him earlier and it went to messaging.

"He's been asked to cover for a colleague. Said he would be home about lunchtime."

Tia said, "Okay, I'll pop over. My sister will come with me, as Alex mentioned you have two adorable cats and she is cat-crazy, if you don't mind. Would Vin mind?"

"No, that's fine. See you later."

"Wow!" Vin couldn't believe how lovely Tia and her sister were. In Vin's experience, nice girls were hard to find, and as a cop working amongst females of all sorts of backgrounds, such as drug abuse, alcohol abuse and physically abused girls, meeting normal, decent and well-spoken girls was a pleasure. Alex was home already, with a face like thunder had a bad day.

"Al, yes, you could say that. Okay, spill. Vin never saw Alex other than bubbly, so something's really bothered you, mate. What is it? When you go back tomorrow, Vin, I will accompany you, as I'm needed to give a verbal statement at the high court. It's the end of a long running trial. I've already given my statement and evidence. I can't believe I'm back again. This is the concluding and sentencing. Then I'm out of there. Alex, I nearly forgot Tia and her sister are coming over after work. Did you get her message? Said she tried to call you. It's okay, mate. She'll be okay. It was too fucking good to be true, me finding heaven in my new home and job, then get called back." Vin had to stay unlike Alex a retreat to get back to. After Alex's mood relaxed, Vin told him of his concerns about Witchy and Soz.

"What's the problem at the bar? I thought everything was going okay."

Vin relayed, "Why the bar has gone quiet?"

"Witchy emailed me, said some roughnecks are scaring the crap out of what customers they have left. Apparently, some hard nuts go into the bar, threatening Witchy and Soz what will happen if they don't get free drinks and push customers around and tables over when they leave. Witchy and Soz aren't martial arts taekwondo experts and are struggling to get regular customers back."

"Do you know what, Vin? The way I'm feeling at the moment, I could do the lot of them in."

"This case has totally rattled me," Vin said.

"Shush, it's Tia and her sister at the door. We can talk later."

Stuck in Vin's mind was the going back to London and leaving this relaxing stress-free retreat behind. Tia's sister was a lovely, lively girl and she wanted to know about Chrissy and Rudi. She seemed to bond with them, and Vin was feeling good. "Don't make them too cosy with you or I'll have to move here because they can be stubborn little blighters."

"This made her laugh. Well, I can't promise. But I'll try."

Vin asked, "By the way, what's your name? All I've heard is Tia's sister and my sister. I can't believe you're nameless."

"Sorry, Vin, it's Zash, short for Zashelle."

"That's a beautiful name and unusual."

Zash explained it came from her Moroccan grandmother. "I wish I was working in London just to feel the buzz."

"Is that how you feel, Vin?"

"Er… yes and no, and since coming here, it's got to be a not, but there are worse places, I suppose. It's okay here, but after the holiday season ends, it goes quiet everywhere." Tia and Alex hugged each other, and until Alex returned, everything carried on as before, and now Zash had a twinkle in her eye and a spring in her step since meeting Vin.

"I take it you like Vin?" asked Tia.

"Yes, he's really nice and decent, but I can't get too carried away. I'm sure London has a zillion of nice girls."

"Don't put yourself down, Zash. If Alex can like me for the way I am, Vin would do the same. Come on let's go shopping. Let the hot cops get packing."

Putting Rudi and Chrissy in the car, Vin said to Alex, "Okay, mate, come back to mine when the hearing is over. See you soon."

"Will do, buddy. Hope it's sooner than later." Getting home from a dream and living the dream like Alex was soon to be changed when an email from Witchy put Vin back into police mode and completely put his brain into first gear. Vin didn't like what he read, and a feeling of sickness in his gut decided whether his new role as a police officer came before his close friends.

"Soz has been put into hospital after an assault and Witchy is helpless to run the bar by himself."

Early evening, there was a knock on Vin's door. Alex looked totally knackered.

"Hi, Al, you look shit."

"Yes, I feel it, and guess what? It looks like the bad guys have guardian angels because the bastard in court today pulled an angelic face, then gets a slap on the wrist. Tell me, Vin, is that real fucking justice? I've had it with policework. My feelings have changed, and after today, I'm putting in my notice."

Vin offered Alex to stay the night as driving late night wasn't sensible.

"Okay I'll just buzz Tia. I don't want her worrying."

The conversation about Witchy began, and between them they discussed how they had been trained and what they could deal with. Vin was absolutely gobsmacked by Alex's revelation that he was a blackbelt in martial arts.

"You kept that one a secret. I thought you were strong and could defend yourself, but wow! You make me feel like a pussy."

"Vin, mate, how would you like to work for me? I'll tell you my plan, but we will need to work out a solution to help your friends and fast."

"Okay, I'm all ears. Shoot. When I've done checks on security firms who include bars and nightclubs, I've got to know door security at most of them and I'm told recently that the boss of one company is selling the business due to personal reasons."

"How could you buy a security firm? You've got to have big money. I know you would be the ideal person to take on such a task. I've got a lump in my throat with how you'd take on something so big to help my friends."

"Thank you, Alex. I'll help you any way I can; just point me in the right direction."

Vin asked, "How would you get the money to invest in this company?"

"Well, Vin, a couple of years ago, my grandmother left a few grand in her will for me. I couldn't believe it myself. She was so kind and you know that saying, 'Keep it for a rainy day.' Well, now it's a rainy day and your friends need help, so what do you say?"

"Do you really want to see me, a grown man cry? Okay, let's do it, but Alex, you will talk this over with Tia. She's really special to you. Don't keep her in the dark. I could tell her I was going to the moon. She would be fine as long as I bought her a gift back. I'll sort it, Vin. Don't worry."

"Alex, what gift could you bring back for her? There's only rock and dust."

"Yes, you dick, that's what she'd get."

"Right. It's ammo time, Vin. Remember when we saw your sarge on that float, of which he doesn't know we know? I said if you need time off for any reason, just use the ammo. You think he has a double, remember?"

Vin said, "Yes, and he'll agree to anything. You got it, use it. One question, Vin, do you want to leave the force because if you don't, I will understand. Vin shook his head no. Alex, this is where I make a stand. Let's do it."

When Vin put his notice in, the sarge couldn't have looked more relieved. He knew Vin had spotted him on the pride float.

"Well, Vin, I'm sorry your career with us is ending. You're a good officer. I hope we can get a replacement with your quality. I wish you well."

Vin had to bite his tongue. 'What a load of lying bollocks!' He was glad to see the back of him. One officer had a big mouth and told of any gossip about anyone. "So sarge, I'll leave knowing you will get the piss ripped out of you and good riddance." The other cops Vin worked with were good guys and promised to keep the community safe and keep him up to date with the sarge. They couldn't help laughing.

"How are we going to look him in the eye now, especially when he is up his own arse. Take care, Vin. Good luck."

Witchy was holding out. He hadn't any idea that Vin and Alex would be there as soon as they could. He messaged Vin to say that at the moment, the bar was quiet and the local cops were keeping an eye out for them. Soz was okay. He just had bruising and was taking it easy. This made Vin feel good, as it wasn't a bus ride to get over to New York.

A phone call to Vin came up with no name; it was Zash.

"Hi, Vin, how are you? When are you visiting Alex? It's so boring, and I miss those darling cats. As soon as I get some personal business sorted, I promise I will come to see you, Tia and Alex. At the moment. my head is full of to-do stuff. If I didn't have the cats to talk to, I'd go mental."

"Thanks for ringing, Zash. I promise to be in touch soon. It's nice to speak to you. Bye for now."

The day before Joe and Roselle's wedding, Raggy asked Vin if he had been in contact with Soz and Witchy.

"Okay, Rags, listen up, and I don't want Joe hearing or knowing this. I don't want to upset him on his special day. It's Witchy's bar; some local lowlife arseholes have been roughing up the place. Also, Soz was hurt, but he's okay. Nothing to worry about. After Joe's wedding tomorrow, you know my friend, ex-cop Alex, well, he is signing a contract to buy a security company. I will be working for him also, as he needs some new staff. I contacted the Leeds' supporter Steve. I asked if any of his friends needed a job. He said big Brad would do anything. He needs some money and is struggling financially. Also, Rags, do you remember him? The really big lad you said you wouldn't mind him manhandling you?"

Raggy smirked, "Oh yes, honey, I remember him, alright. Okay, let's enjoy ourselves tomorrow. Let's see, Joe. Be happy and we will meet up in three days. Make sure your passport is up to date and Alex will lay out the plan so we know what's happening." Joe and Roselle's wedding was sheer heavenly and planned well with a small chair and the

43

'Piece de Resistance', an operatic song performed by a young girl who was Roselle's niece.

Raggy visibly had a tear in his eye. Also, Vin knew that Rudi and Chris would have been invited and loved and lived every breathing moment. As the day wore on, Vin felt it was time to go home and have some wine to finish off. He wished the happy couple good luck and promised a meet up sometime soon.

"What you doing, Rags?"

"Going home and chill."

"I don't think so; I'm over 21."

"Yes, Rags, plus 20. Okay, I'll be in touch in a couple of days. Take care."

Doing some grocery shopping, Vin couldn't believe there were Christmas items around the supermarket, like festive food.

"Oh my goodness, I didn't realise how the year had moved. I haven't got any room in my brain to even think about Christmas yet. Once Witchy and Soz are sorted, I can relax hopefully." The taking over of the security firm went smoothly for Alex, who worried it would take ages. Also, recruiting staff wasn't so difficult after all. "Raggy will have all his dreams come true when he sees the braun and muscle Alex has taken on." One problem Vin had to solve was the cats; he couldn't just leave them. The plan as Alex put it over the phone was something out of a slapstick comedy.

"Did you say I have to act like I'm a gay customer? Are you being serious, Alex?"

"I leave that to the experienced, like Raggy."

"Vin, I'm being serious when we arrive at Witchy's Bar. We will blend in and not let on who or what we are. Just see what's what. Also, big Brad and another muscle man are coming with us and we are staying at the nearest motel so we have quick access to the bar."

"So, get Raggy to give you a quick course in how to act like one of the regulars if they have any left. So, Alex, should I invest in some stiletto heels, some makeup and a few dresses?"

Raggy chipped in, "No, Vin, you can borrow mine."

Vin said, "I've two words for you: fuck off. If and when the hard boys pay a visit, we will sort them once and for all."

Vin had one problem and that was solved when Alex said, "Don't worry. Zash and Tia have booked a day off from work and will drive me to your home pick up the cats, then drop us off at Heathrow. We will meet Brad and Mike there."

This put Vin at ease. Chrissy and Rudi will be fussed over and looked after by Zash. "Thanks, Alex. You've taken a weight off my mind."

"Okay, buddy, see you in two days. Let's get this party started." The flight seemed to drag, and all sorts were sailing through Alex's mind.

Have they gone too far buying this security project? Well, time will tell. Thank god I've got Vin and some decent staff. I just want to nail this problem for Vin's friends once and for all.

Eventually arriving at the motel, Vin messaged Witchy:

"We're here. See you soon."

"Anyone for coffee and doughnuts?"

Brad had noticed the coffeehouse next door.

"Yes, mate. Order some drinks and doughnuts. Be there in a min, and don't eat all the cakes, okay?" Brad promised with a smile.

"I'm on a diet promise not to Raggy, said same as me a seafood diet, everything you see, you eat."

Brad said, "How did you know Raggy? You ain't never been on a diet, so shut it." The coffee shop was welcoming and the regulars were friendly. A small truck parked up and a quietness was felt. Alex eyed the two males entering the café.

He asked, "Vin, did you notice?"

"Yes, I did." He told Brad and Mike to just talk amongst themselves. "And you, Raggy, don't forget we're just passing through, okay? We got the message."

"Oh, look, new customers."

"Don't you mean overgrown cocksuckers as loud as they wanted to be heard. These must be a branch of the long necks bothering Witchy. They obviously are feeling in charge of the area."

"Okay then, are we ready?" asked Alex, and upon standing up, a hand spanned out. "Going already? You haven't introduced yourselves, and that's mighty rude."

Mike and Brad moved closer. "Hi, I'm shotput. This is Javelin."

The males asked, "And why would you be called that?"

With quickness, Brad grabbed the collar of the mouthpiece, paced him out of the cafe and shot-putted him through the air. Then Mike grabbed the front and back of the other and aimed him like a spear in the sky. "Remember our names, won't you?"

Entering the café, everyone clapped. Alex said, "Let's go. The news will get to the ring leaders now."

Vin and Alex apologised to the boss, who said, "Thank you, all. Please call in again and shook hands with everyone. You're quiet, Raggy. Lost your tongue?"

"No, my eyes are still watering after seeing that little showdown." Witchy and Soz were ecstatic on hearing about the new kids on the block.

"So what is the name of your new business, Alex?"

"It's called Pride Secure."

"Oh my Lord, that's brilliant. Are your staff gay smiling?"

Alex replied, "Ask Mike, and if you want to rattle him, I'm sure he won't mind. This is the plan, everyone. If Witchy puts some flyers around advertising, say beer 'n burger night for Saturday, that will give enough time for people to know what's happening at the bar."

Brad asked, "Where do you want us to be – on the door or just circulating?"

Alex said, "Good point; let's see who comes through the door. We will stay vigilant. Then Plan B: if we have to any questions, Raggy asked, 'Do females come to the bar.'"

Soz piped up, "Yes, some are couples, also some straight regulars who are really okay with everyone."

Vin asked, "What about the cops? What's the response time around here?"

A voice from nowhere said, "It depends on how many cops turn up, and the big trouble is you could be beaten to a pulp before the sheriff appears."

Witchy introduced the drag artist. "Everyone, this is Miss Neon."

"Hi, you, all these terrorists need putting in their boxes once and for all." Vin and Alex promised everyone will be okay and no one will get hurt. The grill chef at the coffeehouse offered to cook the burgers and fries for the Saturday evening.

"It will cost you a few beers for my services," he joked.

Witchy said, "Okay, you're on, and thanks." Soz and Witchy asked Vin if they could have a word.

"Yes, sure. What's up?"

"I and Soz have enjoyed running the bar. We've come to New York and have had a great time, but we both feel we would like to go home and settle down. My brother agrees we've done a great job here. In fact, he and his wife and baby also decided to pack up and return to England."

"That's no problem, but what about selling the bar?"

Soz replied, "We're already sorted out the paperwork. It has gone through and we can be out in a week's time. The new owner's plan to have a bar and steakhouse all in one and some refurbishment."

Witchy said, "They know of the problem we've had and are happy to take it on. Okay, I'll tell Alex. Vin was thinking that Christmas is getting nearer and everyone can be home and settled, which reminds me I must give Zash a buzz, see how my little fur balls are doing." Zash was happy to hear from Vin.

"Yes, they are just great. I love them and I've brought them lots of toys. Are you okay, Vin?"

"Yes, and Alex, and myself, plus some others are on a flight home on Sunday evening. I'll be in touch. Take care." Since the incident at the coffeehouse, it was quiet and the atmosphere had changed to calm and there was no sign of anyone intending to cause trouble. Alex checked with Brad and Mike. Raggy and Vin that Saturday night were ready to go. so guys let's bring it on. Customers began to arrive. Brad was more interested in the smell of burger and fries, which everyone was promised at the end of the evening. A female walked to the bar like a regular and ordered a cocktail. She was smiling and talking to Soz like she had been here before. Her eyes scanned around the bar. She must be a local. Then she was chatting to Raggy. The drag artist, Miss Neon, was to perform. Alex and Vin liked her. She couldn't perform or earn money when the roughnecks came in, as they scared everyone away, but tonight, she entered the room with chants of: "We want Neon." The tune of it's raining men put everyone on the dance floor. Suddenly, shouting could be heard, and Brad and Mike took up their positions at the front door and in front of the bar. Raggy grabbed the biggest male and put his hands behind his back while Mike put on the wrist ties. Two others were put to the floor by Vin and Brad, and the sound of police sirens was a relief. The three males were taken outside where two police cars had pulled up and the nice lady who had come into the bar alone and seemed like a regular asked who the in charge was of the security detail.

Alex replied, "That would be me. I've a small security service, of which we are here to help our friends who own the bar. They have endured trouble and damage recently."

The female said, "You've handled it very well."

Alex asked, "Could I ask who you are? I thought you were just a customer."

"Okay, my name is Lara Hurst, or Sheriff Hurst if you like. I've been waiting for these arseholes a while to bang them in jail. Also, I was in the coffeehouse the other day."

Alex said, "Oh no, my guys are going to jail, aren't they?"

With a warm smile, she said, "No, you've really helped me and the people in the area rid these scums, and thank you for dealing with them. You won't be in any trouble. I owe you all a drink."

"Beers all round," said Alex.

She smiled. "I meant a coffee. Once again, thank you, and if ever you want to join my department, there's a place waiting." The evening was enjoyed by all the regulars. Also, Alex had his first security assignment carried out well and the sheriff had praised Alex for the good outcome of a situation, which she promised would not be repeated by the hoodlums. After the bar had closed and the clearing up was all finished, Witchy poured drinks for all Alex's crew.

"Well, cheers everyone. Soz and I will hopefully see you all back home in a week's time. Cheers and thank you all." The motel was a few steps away and the thought of going home was heavenly. Alex and Vin wished everyone goodnight.

"And be up bright and early; we don't want to miss our flight." Vin had a knock on his door and with one eye open, he saw his phone was revealing 6:00 AM.

'No, it can't be morning already.'

Opening the door, he saw Brad Mike and Raggy.

"You said bright and early, so here we are. And no, we didn't shit the bed. We will wait in the reception and get you and Alex a coffee. Our cab has been booked."

"Okay, thanks. Be with you in ten mins." Everyone finished their coffee and the large transporter taxi was prompt and the journey home was a happy thought on seeing family, friends and two fluff balls, Rudi and Chrissy, who Vin missed but knew they were cared for until his arrival. Mike asked how much the cab fare was. The driver refused and said, "Thanks to you guys, my business has picked up. Now the bar is open. I have regular work once again. Thanks and safe journey." A safe journey it was, and Raggy had booked a flight to visit family for Christmas.

"I'll be in touch. Take care and get yourselves home." Brad and Mike decided to stay in London for a couple of days, so Vin and Alex were relieved when they heard a female voice.

"Hi Alex, Vin over here." It was Tia and Zash.

"Wow, you two, we were just checking the underground system."

The girls said, "Come on, we've driven here to collect you both. The weather is rotten at the moment, so let's move it."

Alex gave Tia a big hug and said, "I've missed you so much."

Zash hugged Vin. "Come on. Let's go home." A feeling of being wanted by Zash hit Vin, what with Christmas on the doorstep, who wouldn't want to have another human being to hold, to kiss and feel needed? A quick stop at the motorway services, Zash told of the cats being so cosy and playful and also asked Vin if he would like to do some Christmas shopping with her, of which the answer was a definite, "Oh my God! I haven't got a thing for anyone yet."

Zash would help him and Christmas would be happy and fun. Alex asked if Vin was staying with any family for the festive holiday. "If not, can I suggest you stay at mine? It's Christmas. No one should be alone. Even your cats have each other. Also, we have Tia and Zash to cook, wash up, fill our glasses and…"

"Stop right there." Mr Grinch Tia and Zash were laughing. "We wouldn't have it any other way."

"Vin, are you brave enough to join us for crimbo?"

Alex pleaded to Vin, "Please say yes. I can't handle two feisty women."

Vin's reply was: "Yes, mate. Count me in and thank you." Vin's home was a one-bed apartment and it definitely felt empty, and pressing buttons on the remote control flicking programmes, Christmas Day was a total no-no, and it felt cheerful, the thought of being with Alex and the girls. One day of cleaning a food shop, laundry, then fill up at the garage, then it was all systems go. As promised, Alex, Tia and Zash were ready and, with a coffee, put in his hand. "Come on, buddy, us guys have to shop till we drop, as time is ticking by. So, let's roll."

Vin asked, "Is there a pet shop? I can get something for the cats."

"Don't worry, Vin. I think Zash has spoilt them with goodies."

"Okay, next stop perfume shop inside the shopping mall, so let's get sniffing." Alex mentioned some security work possibly on Christmas Eve.

"Is that okay with you, Vin? Oh, and I'm charging double."

Vin's answer was: "Okay by me. After buying girlie gifts, as Alex put it, I think the girls could be finished gift-buying. Let's go round them up."

Scanning the mall, a wall of bags was moving toward them.

"No, that can't possibly be them. Hell, have they bought the whole shopping mall?"

Vin smiled, "I'd say so, wouldn't you?" Returning to Alex's home, Vin looked at his phone text messages from everyone.

"Joe and Roselle are having a baby; that was quick. Then Raggy, Oh God, don't say he's pregnant. Yo, man! Have a happy Christmas. I'm okay. See you in the new year."

Then,

"Witchy and Soz when you read this, we will be landing at Heathrow. We are both okay. We have a new home. Will let you know more. Take care. Thank you and your friends for your help—Merry Christmas."

Christmas Eve began calm and quiet. Everything Vin could ever want was right here. Then later in the evening, Alex received a phone call; the security team had a problem. When Vin and Alex arrived at a known bar, it was a similar scenario to Witchy's Bar.

"Then a hulk of a male and his side kick pushed Vin and Alex with threats of what you pussy boys going to do. A twist of the heel and an angled turn also a flying kick from Alex, then bang." Alex and Vin physically demonstrated what pussy boys could do.

"Come on, Vin, the security team have cleared them out and my fucking hand is killing me."

"Yeah, and my wrist feels like I've got wanker's cramp but it felt good."

The bar regulars weren't bothered. What had just occurred obviously had come across big. I ams before. But one mature man who was staring at Vin and Alex walked over to them.

"I saw and heard what just took place. Are you both okay?"

Rubbing his hand, Alex said, "Yes, thanks, the security team works for me. I've only just got this contract for the bar. I think I'll be deleted now."

The man introduced himself as Thomas Lar Zechen. "I'm a regular here when I'm in town with my job."

Vin asked, "What's your job?"

The reply was, "Well, I'm a circuit judge and when the local courts are short-staffed, I fill in for a few days, which can I say you two did a fine job on those two shitheads and I've heard of pride secure in the community. Well done, but please don't come before me in court, as I won't be able to praise you. Once again, well done. Let me buy you both a drink. Keep up the good work. Cheers. Do you know what, Vin? I think I vaguely remember the judge from something in the press about some slag who tried it on with a known personality. But the judge put her right back in her shoebox. I remember that as well. She said the person had got her pregnant."

Vin started to giggle. The judge said, "ou only get pregnant if a male has a healthy sperm count, and unfortunately, this person was as sterile as a spoon dipped in bleach. Next."

"Vin, you crack me up. If I remember that, it will be future ammunition. Although I've got plenty of ammo as I'm sure you have. So what's your claim to fame, Alex?"

"Well, I did college and I've got an ology."

"Oh, so you're clever and got what ology after your name."

"Alex, you're drunk, please tell me."

"Okay, it's a poo-ology." Vin couldn't think what that was.

"Okay, what's that?"

"It means my head is full of shit."

"Vin, let's move it."

"Alex, where has the year gone? It's been good, bad, rough and rocky, but we've both survived. I'm happy you're happy. You've landed on terra firma with your new job and home and lovely Tia."

"Yes, Vin, we need to prepare ourselves because lovely Tia and Zash could give us a kick in the balls when we return home and that worries me, but we are a team, and as they say, all for one and one for all, Merry Christmas."